Finding Beauty in Disaster 2

A Novel

Written by Allison Searson

Finding Beauty in Disaster 2
ISBN: 9781736745564

www.one2mpower.com
Editor Shawn Jackson
Illustration by Yuly Raquel
Cover Design by Design Place LLC
Printed in the United States of America 2021

Acknowledgments

I would like to thank God, Jehovah Jireh, my provider, for providing me with the tools, strategies, and ideas for this book. Without God, none of what I'm doing would be possible.

A huge shout out to my sister, parents, and entire family for always covering me in prayer, walking this faith journey with me, having my back, and supporting me like crazy. It means the world to me, and I LOVE YOU ALL!

A special thanks to my grandfather, Elder James Lucas Sr., who has gone on to be with Jesus. He always poured into me and spoke life over the things God showed him concerning me. I miss him tremendously, but I cherish every memory I have of him.

A very special thank you to my amazing publisher Robin Major-Oliphant of One2Mpower Publishing, for helping to bring my vision to life. Did I mention that she's amazing?! Thanks so much for everything.

And last but certainly not least, I want to thank all my supporters for supporting me, purchasing my materials, and for walking this faith journey with me. Thanks for inquiring about part two! Tell a friend to tell a friend about all the amazing things God is doing. I love you all. To God be all the glory. We only goin' up from here! As my sister, Alyssa and her best friend Bryson say, "Lord my! Look at Him worketh!"

XOXO,
Allison

"To all who mourn in Israel, he will give a crown of beauty for ashes, a joyous blessing instead of mourning, festive praise instead of despair. In their righteousness, they will be like great oaks that the Lord has planted for his own glory."

Isaiah 61:3 (NLT)

"And he shall be like a tree planted by the rivers of water, that bringeth forth his fruit in his season; his leaf also shall not wither; and whatsoever he doeth shall prosper."

Psalms 1:3 (KJV)

He's trading beauty for your ashes.
He's planting your roots deep.

Introduction

Most of you may know me and my story, but for those of you who don't, allow me to reintroduce myself. Hi, my name is Natasha. I had it all, lost it, and then gained more than I've ever had before. People say I have the patience of Job. I've been through so much, but through it all, God has been faithful. Sometimes I forget and allow the weight of the world to come crashing down on my shoulders, although I was never meant to handle or carry any of it. This new season has been a lot for me, and I do mean A LOT! Things got too heavy to where I was depleted emotionally, physically, and mentally. I was here (alive), but I wasn't here. I was mentally checked out because I had too much going on, too much to deal with and handle on my own. BUT once I realized I'm not God, I gave it all to Him, and He took care of me. He really did! Walk on this journey with me and see how, yet again, God traded beauty for my ashes.

Prologue

I haven't had the best of luck with love, being how my first marriage ended, but I'm grateful God gave me another chance at it. Tyler and I are getting married, and at first, I thought this wouldn't happen because of the whole Rhonda situation. I thought he was too fickle, but he truly bossed up, and now we're getting ready to spend the rest of our lives together. But during this joyous occasion, something terrible happened. It was completely unexpected, well, at least to me anyway.

When this terrible, awful thing happened to my family and me, I felt like part of me died. I've experienced a lot of hurt and pain before, but not like this! I needed every bit of Jesus to help me to get through this and guess what? He did! He comes through every single time. So, come along with me on my journey to see how God, yet again, traded beauty for my ashes.

CHAPTER ONE
The Wedding

May 10, 2002 was one of the happiest days of my life! On this day, I married the love of my life—Tyler Washington. I know you may be confused because I told you he was fickle because of the whole Rhonda situation, but guess what? He bossed up. He quit listening to other people and listened to what God was telling him. He became the leader I knew he could be all along. He pursued and loved me like Christ pursues and loves His church. He not only fell in love with me, but he fell in love with my kids. He was a great role model for my boys, and Taylor was his absolute world. Mind you, at the time, he didn't have any kids of his own, but he *always* treated my kids like they were his flesh and blood.

Now, back to May 10, 2002. It was a beautiful day, warm and sunny. The church was filled with the ones we loved; well, most of them because Tyler's family opposed him being in a relationship, let alone marrying a woman who had three kids. Anywho, back to the wedding. The church was decorated beautifully with my favorite colors: lilac, mint green, pale yellow, and coral. My parents looked at me in awe as they prepared to walk me down the aisle for the LAST time. I remember looking into my father's eyes and immediately noticing something wasn't right; even the way he felt when he touched me wasn't right.

"You look absolutely beautiful, baby girl. I'm so proud of how far you have come in the Lord," Daddy said.

I began to gaze into his eyes and examine him even further. "Daddy, is everything alright? Are you feeling okay?" I asked.

Mama looked shocked and stared at both of us. Daddy hesitated to answer me and said, "I'm alright, baby girl...everything will be okay. Focus on your special day."

Something about Daddy still didn't sit well with me. I could tell something was wrong, but he insisted he was fine, and I should focus on marrying the love of my life.

The church doors swung open as it was time for me to walk down the aisle. My eyes immediately met Tyler's. He was crying when he saw me. How sweet! I looked at my children standing beside him and all the people in the congregation. I was overwhelmed with joy, yet I did not have a peace about my father.

Our wedding ceremony was beautiful; it was an absolute dream. Then I, Tyler, the kids, and our wedding party headed outside to take pictures while everyone else headed straight to the reception. I did notice Aaron didn't show up. He told me he wasn't coming, but he also told the kids he would be here to see them because they were in the wedding. It didn't bother me one bit, but it bothered them because, and I quote, "Daddy said he would come!" Nevertheless, it was a spectacular day.

It came time for us to be introduced as Mr. and Mrs. Tyler Washington at the reception. When we walked in, there were lots of cheers and expressions of joy. Then it happened. We heard a loud thud and a scream of horror coming from the direction where my parents were.

The music stopped, which brought everything to a halt. I immediately rushed over to my parents to see what was going on. I laid eyes on my daddy lying on the ground. "DADDY!" I screamed. He had passed out on the floor. Immediately we dialed 9-1-1 as we checked his breathing and made sure he still had a pulse. I gazed into my mother's eyes. "This *cannot* be happening! This was supposed to be the best day of my life," I said to her. She tried to reassure me everything would be okay with Daddy, but she just looked scared and nervous. It was almost as if she knew something that I didn't know.

After what felt like an eternity, the paramedics finally arrived. They wheeled Daddy out on a stretcher and loaded him into the ambulance. Forget the wedding reception, we immediately got into our cars and followed behind.

"Tyler, I can't believe this is happening! Daddy has been the healthiest person I've ever known. What could possibly be wrong with him?"

"I don't know, Babe; all we can do is pray it's something minor, and he'll be back to feeling like his old self in no time."

"But what I don't get is why Mama looked like she knows something I don't know. What could she possibly have to hide?"

Tyler got a little fidgety at this remark. *Does he know something that I don't know too?*

The waiting room in a hospital is not where I thought I would be on my wedding day. But there I was in my white, poofy wedding gown, pacing back and forth because I could not sit still. It felt like my mind was going a million miles a minute. "What's wrong with Daddy, and will he be okay?" were the thoughts that flooded my head. Tyler grabbed me and said, "Tasha, Dad is going to be okay; you just have to trust God and have faith." Then he held me close, and I felt his heartbeat, which made me trust him all the more. In his arms, I felt secure, and I believed him. Yeah, I believed him, but even more than that, I believed God.

CHAPTER TWO
The Truth

We were finally able to go to Daddy's room to see him. Since Mama was already back there, only two could go back at a time, so Darrell and I went back to see him.

"Daddy!"

"Hey, baby girl. Hey Darrell."

"Pop, you sure gave us a scare. How you feelin'? You alright?"

"Boy, they got me hooked up to all this stuff, how you think I'm doing."

"Daddy, you gone be alright? What did the doctor say?" I asked.

Mama and Daddy kind of stared at each other, and then they both looked at me. Darrell turned his face to the wall.

"What did he say? Daddy is one of the healthiest people that I know. It can't be that bad, right? No matter what it is, God is Jehovah Rapha. He'll heal you, Daddy. I know He will."

"Baby girl, I'm so proud of how far you've come and how much you've grown in the Lord and in your faith in Him. I've fought a good fight, I've kept the faith, and I did everything God told me to do, but I'm tired now. I'm tired."

What does he mean he's "tired"? What's going on? At this point, both Darrell and Mama were staring at the ground, and Daddy was staring at the ceiling. It was almost as if he was seeing Heaven. God, I'm so confused! This doesn't sound like my daddy at all. My daddy would be encouraging himself to keep fighting. He would be preaching and quoting scripture right now. What has changed? Did I miss something?

"But I don't understand, Daddy...could someone please tell me what's going on?

"Tasha—"

"No, Darrell. I need to be the one to tell her," Daddy said.

"Baby girl, there's something I've been keeping from you...and I wanted to tell you, but I wasn't sure of the right time. But I guess now is as good a time as any...I have stage four cancer. I've known for quite some time, but I didn't tell you because of everything you were going through."

Tears started to stream down my face. Darrell held me as Daddy spoke.

"You were just starting to find God again, re-establishing your relationship with Him, starting a new relationship with Tyler, and figuring out your life. I didn't think it would be a good time to tell you because I wasn't sure if you could handle it in the vulnerable state you were in. I couldn't do that to you then; it would've been too much."

"Daddy. this is too much to hear right now!" I said.

"I'm sorry this had to happen on your wedding day. Believe me; I wanted nothing more than for this to be the best day of your life— a joyous celebration and occasion. I'm so proud of the woman you are and the woman of God you're still becoming. You're much stronger than I think you are. You're stronger than YOU think you are. Focus on God, raising those precious babies, and your new life with Tyler. Don't worry about me, baby girl. Don't worry about me."

"Daddy, you're the pillar of this family! You're the one that always keeps us together, the glue of this family. You cannot give up! That's not an option for you! You gotta be here to see your sons get married. You gotta be here to see your grandbabies grow up. You gotta be here. I need you to be here, Daddy!
I NEED YOU HERE!" I sobbed.

"Baby girl, it's all about God's timing. He's been more than faithful to me and to this family. No doubt I'll be here as long as God wants me to be here, but baby girl, I'm tired. I'M TIRED."

The doctor walked in to speak with my parents. I tried to quickly dry all of my tears.

"Hi guys, I'm Dr. Smith, and I'll be working with you all. Oh wow, you all are definitely looking spiffy! What's the occasion?" Dr. Smith asked.

"My baby girl got married today," Daddy said.

"Wow! Congratulations! Now we just gotta get your dad fixed up so you guys can be on your way," Dr. Smith said nervously.

"Do you guys mind stepping out while I speak to your parents?" Dr. Smith asked.

"No problem," Darrell said as he grabbed my hand to leave the room.

I didn't want to leave Daddy. I wanted to stay. I couldn't believe what was happening. I couldn't believe he was just now telling me about this. If I'd known, I would've prayed harder for him; I would've made sure to cover him daily, not just whenever he crossed my mind. How couldn't I have seen the signs?! I guess I needed to do what I knew to do: pray.

God, You've gotta heal my daddy! Please, God, he's been faithful to You. Don't let me down, God, come through for my daddy. Come through for my daddy, God. He's done right by You and his family. Please heal him and show Yourself mighty and strong. In Jesus' name, amen.

I know God will come through for Daddy; I just know He will. We walked
back to the waiting room where everyone was anxiously awaiting a report.

"Well, what did the doctor say?" AJ asked.

"We don't know, he asked us to leave the room so he could speak to Ma and Pop in private," Darrell answered.

"This don't look good," Trey said.

"Not at all," Travis chimed in.

Scott just sat in his chair fiddling with his fingers looking worried, "Pop ain't ever look that bad before, dawg. All of them other times he was able to pull through. Y'all think he gone make it?" he asked.

"Pop's a trooper, of course he gone make it! What the heck kind of question is that?!" AJ said.

"Hold up, 'all of them other times.' WHAT OTHER TIMES?!" "What do you mean, 'other times'?! Did y'all know Daddy had cancer?!" I asked.

They all held their heads down. Tyler looked at my brothers, and then he walked towards me. "Baby, they just wanted to shield and protect you is all," he said.

"WHAT?! You knew about this too?! WHY DIDN'T ANYONE THINK TO TELL ME?! Don't you think as his daughter I deserved to know?" I asked.

"Bae—"

"Don't even," I said.

"Man, it ain't like we wanted to leave you hangin' in the dark. Pop ain't want us to tell you," Travis said. "He wanted to protect you because he really thought this would pass, and he'd get better."

"He didn't want you to worry about him, sis," Darrell said.

At this point, I didn't know what to say or do. I just needed to be alone with God, so I went into any empty corner to try and gather my thoughts. I can't believe *nobody* told me about this! I can't believe Tyler knew and didn't tell me! We just got married; we can't be starting off with secrets! That's not a good way to start off our marriage! *How long has Daddy been sick? Why did I have to find out this way on my wedding day? Why didn't anyone trust me enough to tell me the truth?!*

CHAPTER THREE
Pain

It's been about four weeks since Daddy has been in the hospital, and I have been visiting him all day, every day, but today was different. When I got to his room, the door was wide open. Mama was sitting in the chair like she always had been for the past four weeks, but today she was weeping.

"Mama?" I said as I walked into the room.

She looked up at me and continued weeping. My brothers were all standing around. Tyler grabbed my hand as we walked into the room, and I immediately noticed Daddy, nor his bed, were in the room.

"Where's Daddy? He should be out of surgery by now," I said. Deep down, I knew, but I just didn't want to believe it.

"Um...Tasha, I always try to be gentle with you, but I really don't know how to say this," Darrell said.

"NO! NO! NO! Don't even say it! It can't be true! It CAN'T be!"

Tyler held me close.

"You know Pop had to have emergency surgery this morning. He didn't make it through the surgery."

"NO!"

They're going to wheel him in any moment now!"

I sobbed.

"Baby, he's in a better place," Mama said as she grabbed me.

"I didn't get to say goodbye or tell him I loved him one last time."

"I know, baby. I know. But your daddy knew you loved him," Mama said as we sobbed together.

We all sat in Daddy's hospital room for what seemed like an eternity before we decided to head over to what's now just Mama's house to plan something I never, ever expected to have to plan: Daddy's funeral. I hate the thought of him not walking through those doors again. I thought I knew pain, but man, this was the worst! I can't believe on June 7, 2002, I lost my absolute very best friend. This was by far the hardest thing I've ever had to endure because he wasn't coming back (at least not in this lifetime).

June 14, 2002 was one of the hardest days of our lives. That was the day we laid to rest my best friend. For it to have been a summer day, it sure was gloomy. Dressed in all black; black shoes, black dress, black hat, and sadness all over my face. Tyler held the boys on his lap as their faces screamed hurt, sadness, and pain, while he tightly held my hand. Young Taylor didn't understand what was happening and wanting to play because she saw a field of green grass. It was hard for them to understand their Pop-Pop was not going to come back.

My brothers. Oh, God, my brothers! Daddy was the glue that held them together. Despair was written all over their faces. God help them! SAVE them! And oh, my precious mother. I couldn't help but weep for her. She lost her love, the *only* man she'd ever known. She wept bitterly as she touched my father's hand and kissed his forehead oh so sweetly for the last time.

I couldn't bear to watch them lower him into the ground. I just couldn't come to terms with it. I wept as Tyler held the kids and I close. My brothers tried to put on a front and act hard, but they couldn't keep it together. I've never seen them so broken, bare, and raw. They were all wailing. *God help us! There's no way we can make it through this without You!*

Mama was given a lot of support from the church, which was much needed. The funeral was over, but not for us. I tried to put a smile on my face at the repass, but I just couldn't front, I just wanted to go home. Daddy and I were so close that when he died, it felt like part of me died with him. I'm grateful for the time we had; I just wish I could've held him tighter, longer.

Tyler had been the real MVP. He spent the first month of our marriage in the hospital with Daddy, taking care of the kids when I didn't have the strength to do it, covering me and my family in prayer, and being my support system. I really thank God for him; he was Heaven sent.

"Babe, you're Heaven sent. You've held it down for the kids, supported me, and you've been faithful to help Daddy in any way you could. God's *definitely* going to bless you," I said.

"I do what I can, and I'll never stop doing. God, you, and the kids are my priority. As long as I got breath in me, I got y'all," he said before kissing me.

"Ew," Corbin and Calvin said, and we both couldn't help but laugh.

"At least the kids will get to take their minds off of Daddy aka Pop-Pop by spending time with their dad," I said.

"Yeah. Have you heard from Aaron yet? Because he's not responding to any of my calls or texts," Tyler said.

"He knows we buried Daddy today, so maybe he's giving us time with family?" I suggested.

But in reality, we both knew how Aaron was; we just didn't want to say it in front of the kids.

"I'll call him once we're home," I said.

Once the repass was over, it was time for us to go home. So that Mama wouldn't be returning to a big, lonely house, we offered for her to come and stay with us. She declined because she wanted to be in her own house, so Darrell and Scott opted to go stay with her for a while, which was so sweet of them.

Once we got home, we wound down, settled the kids, and decided to call Aaron. The phone rang for an eternity.

"Hello?" Aaron said.

"Hey Aaron, how are you?" I asked.

"I'm actually kind of busy at the moment, so could we speed this up?" he said.

RUDE! He ain't even ask how I'm feeling about burying my daddy!

"Okay...I'll make it quick. I just wanted to touch bases with you and figure out when you're picking up the kids to spend time with them?" I asked.

I hear silence, "Aaron?!"

"Yeah, Um...Tasha, I'm here."

"The kids are really looking forward to y'alls time together, and I really think it'll take their minds off of losing their Pop-Pop for a bit."

"Yeah, about that...something came up, and I ain't gone be able to do it."

Frustrated, Tyler grabbed the phone from me.

"Yeah, this is Tyler. What do you mean you 'ain't gone be able to do it'? Corbin, Calvin, and Taylor are your children, and they're counting on you! You're always making empty promises to them. Don't you understand you're missing the most precious moments and years of their lives?! Some men would die to have what you have, bro, and you've completely taken it for granted; you've lost sight of what's important."

"Yeah...Buddy... um, who made you Mr. Know-it-all?" Aaron mocked.

"I hate to break it to you 'Buddy,' but I've been more of a father to them than you have. You really need to step it up! If not, they'll grow up to resent you, and it'll be too late. Trust me; I know firsthand cause I was that kid. I hated my dad because he wasn't there for me. I don't want that for Corbin, Calvin, and Taylor, but that's on you, homie."

"Okay, who put the wife stealer on the phone?!" Aaron yelled.

"Bro, are you serious?!" Tyler asked.

I grabbed the phone from Tyler.

"Cut the crap, Aaron! I just buried my father, for goodness sake. Are you picking up the kids this weekend or not?"

"No! I told you something came up and I ain't gone be able to do it. I'm sorry about your dad and all, but I gotta go! I'll call YOU, not the wife stealer, next week. Bye!" Aaron said before the phone clicked off.

I can't deal with Aaron and his foolishness right now! Doesn't he know I literally just buried my dad less than twelve hours ago?! Doesn't he know his kids miss him, and he causes them pain and disappointment with every empty promise he makes? Doesn't he know we're grieving and in pain. Does he even care? I don't have time for him. No devil! Not today Satan, NOT tuhday.

CHAPTER FOUR
Too Soon

It's been about three months since we buried Daddy, and the wound is STILL fresh. It seems like it was just yesterday he was lying in that hospital bed and then gone. With everything that happened, Tyler and I didn't even have a chance to go on our trip for our honeymoon. I felt really bad about that, but too much was happening all at once; too much for me to handle. I promised him I'd make it up to him, but I'm not sure how or when I'll be able to follow through on that promise.

I've been here (alive), *but I haven't really been here.* I've been doing my normal everyday stuff, but just going through the motions. I'm emotionally, mentally, and physically depleted. My body hasn't felt right these last couple of weeks. Everybody's looking to me; it's like they're counting on me to show strength based off everything I've been through and endured. Mama, my brothers, husband, and kids are all looking to me. They're depending on me, and I can't help but feel like I've let them down. I'm a mere human for goodness sake! Shouldn't they be looking to God anyway?!

I don't have the energy to do anything. I'm surrounded by people, yet I feel isolated and alone. This loss really hit me; it took a toll on me. My daddy was my homie, my best friend. We were two peas in a pod. I actually think I was closer to him than to Mama, but I don't love her any less. I think part of all of us died when Daddy died. It's like there's a void in my chest. If that wasn't worse enough, it's like all those wounds are freshly ripped open every time I look at and go near the church. Daddy's blood, sweat, and tears went into that church as he, with the help of God, built it from the ground up. That building was his blueprint, his God-inspired ideas. I hate the thought of some stranger coming in to take over. No sooner than that thought left my mind, Mama called. I could hear her crying.

"Mama, what's wrong?!"

"It seems like your daddy just been put in the ground, and they already tryna replace him," she whimpered.

"What do you mean?! Everyone agreed we'd wait six months and hear from God to figure out who would be the new pastor and all of that. It was my understanding that Daddy's assistant, Pastor Dawson, would continue to lead until we took care of finding a new senior pastor. Pastor D said he didn't want to take on that role but would help in any way he could."

"That was the understanding! But apparently, some of the church folks been holding meetings behind Pastor Dawson *and* our backs!"

WHAT?! Who would do such a thing? Who would go behind our backs and start stirring up mess and confusion?!

"Ma, you gotta be kidding me! Who would do that?" I asked.

"Baby girl, you know just as good as I do who's behind all this mess."

I began to think. *Who would do this?* Then it hit me. It hit me like a ton of bricks...RHONDA! She's always hated me and had it out for me. She hated me even more since Tyler and I got married. But I didn't think she'd be that much of an insensitive jerk to do something like this while we're *still* grieving Daddy's loss and while the church is still grieving the loss of their beloved pastor and shepherd of thirty-two years. She can't be that wicked, *or can she?*

"Baby girl, you still there?"

"I'm here... I was just trying to process."

"Um-hum, that ole Tina and her Rhonda were always starting mess," Mama said before I cut in.

"I don't mean to cut you off, Ma, but for some reason, she's always hated me. Ever since we were kids, she'd try to get the other girls in the church not to like me and then hated them because they did like me. It didn't matter what I did; the girl always hated me, even more now since Tyler and I got married."

"The spirit of jealousy is real and heavy with that one. She learned it at a young age. It ain't nothin' you ever did baby that made her not like you. Her whole family has always been that way. Rhonda learned it from her mama, and her mama learned it from her mama, and so forth. That was one of the families that were always causing disharmony and discord, but your daddy and I and other strong members in the church just kept praying and praying, and eventually just about all of 'em left *except* Rhonda and her mama, Tina."

"My God, my Lord. Lord my!"

"Um-hum. Pastor D said one of the elders told him there's a meeting going on at the church today at noon. I want to be there so I can get down to the bottom of this, and I want you to come with me too. I'd ask your brothers, but you and I both know their minds ain't no good. Well, maybe Darrell, but I don't feel like dealing with all that today."

"Alright, Ma. I'll pick you up, and we'll go together. Love you, see you soon."

"Love you too, baby."

As soon as I hung up with Mama, Tyler walked into the room.

"Morning baby, the kiddos are at school, and I made you some breakfast."

He's so sweet, but I haven't had much of an appetite for the last few days.

"Thanks, babe, but I'm not really hungry."

"You haven't been eating for the last couple of days, and I'm concerned about you. You need to at least try to eat something, or we're going to get you checked out at the doctors."

"There's some secret meeting at the church we're not supposed to know about, but we do know about, and Mama wants me to pick her up and take her," I said, as a means to distract him from thinking about me not eating.

Tyler looked a bit confused at hearing "secret meeting." Then he said, "Alright, I'll drive you both and go with you, *after* you eat at least a little bit of your breakfast," he said as he held the plate out in front of me.

I grabbed the plate. I know the food was clean and safe to eat, but for some reason, the aroma and smell just made me sick, and it felt like I was going to vomit. I started gagging.

"Baby, are you okay?" he asked with a concerned look on his face.

"I'm just all out of sorts. My head hurts, and I really can't eat, nor do I want to right now...maybe it's because of everything we're going through right now. I'll just drink some water, and I'll be fine. Maybe I need to fast and pray more because I haven't been doing that as much since Daddy died."

Tyler was examining me and seemed unsure of what to do.

"I'm okay, I promise." *At least I hoped I'd be okay.*

"I'll take your word for it, but I'm still booking you a doctor's appointment," he said as we got in the car and headed to Mama's house.

CHAPTER FIVE
D-O-N-E, Done!

We pulled up to Mama's house to find her sitting on her porch, anxiously awaiting my arrival.

"Mama Cooper, why are you sitting out here in the heat? It's too hot for you to be out here," Tyler said as he hugged Mama.

I LOVE their relationship.

"Boy, I had to get out of there because y'alls brothers are 'bout to drive me crazy!" she said as she hugged me. Then she looked closely at me and said, "Baby girl, are you feeling okay? You don't look like yourself."

"She hasn't been eating lately, and even the smell of food makes her gag," Tyler chimed in.

Mama looked concerned.

"You ain't mention none of this when we talked on the phone earlier. You gonna see a doctor?" Mama looked at me questioningly.

"I didn't mention it because I'm fine...just been going through it since losing Daddy and all. I'm sure I'm fine, and you all might just be overreacting. God's got me; I know He does."

"Yeah, we know God's got you. But you still have to use wisdom and take care of yourself. That's why He allowed for there to be doctors and nurses. GO SEE ONE," she said.

"That's what I've been telling her, Ma," Tyler interjected.

I rolled my eyes because I felt like they were overreacting. Everyone deals with grief and loss differently, right? I mean, our bodies handle things differently.

"Girl, don't you be rollin' them eyes at me. You ain't too old for a beatin'. I'll put you over my knee and give you a good ol' whoopin' in front of your husband," she chuckled.

I laughed and said, "I just think it's no big deal, and you guys are overreacting, is all. I appreciate you both for being concerned, but I'll be fine. I promise," I said.

"Um-hum. Y'all get grown and then can't tell ya nothin'." But Imma leave you in the hands of the Lord. Now, let's go before your brothers figure out I'm gone."

We were approaching the car as my brothers were coming out of the house.

"Mama, you tryna slip away and ain't tell nobody?" AJ asked.

"Ain't even tell us Tasha and Tyler were here," Scott said.

My brothers proceeded to dap Tyler up and hug me.

Where y'all goin'? We ain't invited?" Travis asked.

Mama, Tyler, and I all looked at each other.

"Tasha, you okay? Lookin' all pale in the face. Look like you lost some weight since I saw you last week!" Trey said.

"Y'all, I promise I'm fine. Everybody handles, experiences, and deals with things differently," I said.

"So... you've been starving yourself?" AJ asked.

"No! I have not been starving myself. I just haven't felt like eating is all. Besides, I need to fast and pray to deal with y'all and the loss of Daddy."

"To each his own," Scott said.

"Anyway, back to the original question. Where are y'all going?" Travis asked.

Mama looked at us and shook her head. There was an awkward silence, and then Darrell spoke, "They're going to the church," he said.

We all looked at him. How did he know that? Did he overhear me and Mama talking? There's no other way he could know that unless he heard it from God himself.

"You must've overheard me on the phone," Mama said.

"No. I literally heard it just now. Like, it popped in my spirit," Darrell said.

Mama looked at him in disbelief. I mean, we had been praying my brothers would get saved and hear from God for themselves. Did she not believe her own prayers? Did I not believe because when he opened his mouth to tell us where we were going, it didn't cross my mind that God would've revealed that to him? I wonder what else God's been telling him that we don't know about.

"Well, the Holy Spirit must've told you then because that's exactly where we're going."

AJ, Scott, Travis, and Trey looked confused.

"Why are y'all going to the church? We already got all of Pop's stuff out," Trey said.

"I didn't even want to tell y'all because I know how y'all are. We're going to the church because apparently there have been secret meetings going on behind our backs about who our new shepherd should be."

"I thought—"

"Hush Travis and let me finish. Yes, we were supposed to all be in prayer about it. But some church thugs got a group together and are wreaking havoc. So, we were going to pop up at the meeting to find out what is going on for ourselves," Mama said.

"For some reason, I feel like I should be there too," Darrell said.

"And you already know we comin' too," AJ chimed in.

Mama rolled her eyes but didn't resist them coming with us. We piled into her van and headed to the church. Everyone was quiet the entire ride. I felt like maybe we should pray so we wouldn't operate in the flesh. Romans 7:18 tells us no good thing dwells in the flesh. What I want to do, I don't do, and the things I don't want to do, I do. The spirit within us is *always* willing, but the flesh is so fickle and weak man! I wanna do right; be gentle and kind to Rhonda, but I have a feeling she gone say the wrong thing to me, and I'm gone want to throw some hands. I ain't fight since I was in like middle school, but I have a feeling I'll do it today if she steps to me in a way that I don't like. This seemed like the *longest* ride ever!

"Hey guys, I think we should pray before we get to the church...and I'm willing to lead us in prayer," Darrell said.

WHAT?! Darrell praying and leading prayers now?! Okay, God! You're doing something NEW and MAJOR! Mama looked surprised.

"Alright, son, gone pray then," she said.

"Alright, let's close our eyes and bow our heads. Except you, Tyler, because you're driving," Darrell said as he proceeded to pray.

Dear Heavenly Father, I thank You for this day, this moment, this space, and this time. Father, I thank You for my family being with me and the time You gave us with Daddy. God, we are unsure of what to expect once we enter this meeting, but YOU ARE SURE. You see all and You know all, so we ask that You'd go before us. Let us remain calm, behave in a Godly manner, represent You well, and show respect to others NO MATTER how they treat us. You're the ONLY One we want to hear and please. What concerns You, concerns us. You're not the author of confusion. You, God, bring about peace, and You tell us that in 1 Corinthians 14:33. What hurts You hurts us, and we desire for your desires to be fulfilled. Let us not operate in the flesh, but in the Spirit. The spirit is willing, but the flesh is weak. Let the Holy Spirit reign supreme and take control of us. In Jesus' mighty name, we pray. Amen.

We all said amen. After Darrell's prayer, his eyes were still closed, and he was whispering. It almost sounded like he said, "And Father, if it be your will, allow this cup to pass from me." He wept a little but quickly dried his tears. He looked out of the van window for the rest of the ride to the church.

I *always* knew Darrell was different from my other brothers. But after he offered up that prayer, I could tell a shift had taken place in his life. Maybe he could be *the one*?

After what seemed like an eternity, we finally arrived at the church to see a lot of cars in the parking lot. Just as Mama and I had suspected, both Rhonda and her mama were there. Pastor D said he would meet us at the church, and we all walked in together. Daddy's office door was open, and it looked like someone was rummaging through his papers. The sanctuary doors were also open. It was clear they were not trying to hide whatever it was that they were doing. Rhonda and her mama were at the front of the church. We walked in, and I could hear Tina saying, "How long are we going to continue going without an official shepherd. Pastor Cooper was a good pastor, God rest his soul, but he's no longer here. We've got to move on. Pastor Dawson does the best he can, I guess, but he's no Pastor Cooper. We can't wait on them to decide and make up their mind about what they gone do. Our souls are at stake, and we *need* a new Godly leader. I've done my research and even looked through some of Pastor Cooper's stuff in his office and found some information on local pastors and some of his old pastor friends. Maybe one of them can take over for us."

Both she and Rhonda looked up at us as we walked in. They had a wicked smirk on their faces. Although the prayer just went forth, AJ had no chill.

"Pop built this church with God, his blood, sweat, and tears. You talkin' bout you need this and need that, and being completely insensitive to not only our emotions and feelings but to the members who *actually* loved and cared about him. I know I ain't really been much of a churchgoer, but I'm pretty sure it don't work like this. You don't just randomly decide on your own who your new pastor should be; you should be praying with us and trying to consult God."

Pop off then, AJ!

"How can you respond, and you're not one hundred percent sure of what we've done," Rhonda chimed in, but then AJ cut her off.

"And how dare you put your mouth on Pastor Dawson. HOW DARE YOU?! This man is much like my pop, a man after God's heart. He's an excellent leader, and ain't no doubt in my mind God walks with him. You need to STAY IN YOUR LANE and stop trying to stir up mess. All these folks listenin' to y'all are out of place and out of alignment. Trust me; you don't want it.

YOU DO NOT WANT IT WITH US! You don't want no smoke wit' us."

"This is why we didn't want you all to know we were holding meetings in the first place. Who told you anything anyway?!" Rhonda asked.

"Well, newsflash, if ya didn't want us to know about what you were doing, then you shouldn't have been meeting here at the church in the first place!" Travis said.

"I'm just really disappointed you all would plot and scheme and try to take matters into your own hands when we've already consulted God, and He already told us what we should do. God said to allow Pastor Dawson to lead us, be in prayer, and in SIX MONTHS, *HE* would send us a leader," Mama said.

"Really?! Cuz we, Rhonda and I, didn't hear that. I don't think God would want us to wait *that* long for a new permanent leader," Tina said.

I know this heifer didn't—

"AJ is right! You all are out of order and alignment with God and His plan. He's already given those in leadership instruction. We are following His instruction and way and listening for His voice through fasting and prayer. You're leading people who are hungry for God and trying to do right astray, and for that, you should be ashamed. You have no right to be carrying on the way you are, and it is very disrespectful how you not only invaded the Coopers' privacy by rummaging through Pastor Coopers things, but you also left his office in shambles. You know exactly what you're doing. You're treading on dangerous ground. If I were you, I'd do a complete 360, repent and turn around," Pastor Dawson said.

"Pastor Dawson, with all due respect, I really don't think you know what you're talking about," Tina said. "How you gone lead people and be in charge when you said it yourself you didn't want to do it in the first place. If you're unsure of yourself, how you gone expect us to be sure of you? You can't lead others that way. I've said it once, and I'll say it a thousand times if need be, we *need* a new leader, and we need one now! All in favor, say aye."

Those sitting in the congregation said, "Aye." Both Tina and Rhonda got really close to us. Rhonda then whispered, "It's all of us against you. What you gone do? We've got them wrapped around our fingers, and we *will* have this church and get you all out of our way."

I felt my hand lift to smack her, but Tyler grabbed it and held it. Then Darrell said, "We ain't gone have to do nothin' because God is fighting for us. You're treading on dangerous ground leading all of these people astray, as

Pastor Dawson said. But God will get the glory, and His will will be done. Ain't no doubt about it. You think you're standing in our way, but you're really standing in God's way. You can both repent and turn away from this, and all your other sins or God will deal with you. You don't want Him to because He'll move you out of the way. Don't even worry about it family. It's gone all work out and be alright. Let's bounce."

Pastor Dawson confiscated their keys (not sure how they got them in the first place) and made them all leave. We cleaned up Daddy's office before leaving. I really can't believe this is happening; I really can't. I knew Tina and Rhonda were wicked, but I didn't know they had this in them. I mean this was a new level of low. At this point, I'm beyond done with them; D-O-N-E, done!

CHAPTER SIX
Not Again!

All that mess with Rhonda, Tina, and the church has me feeling even worse! I've been trying to let on that I've been fine, but nobody has been buying it. I've had a lot of quiet time with God lately, and He's really been healing me emotionally, mentally, and spiritually. I've been asking Him to heal me physically, but He hasn't done that YET. I still haven't been eating like I want to; the only thing I can keep down is liquids. I guess it's just one of those things I have to experience and go through right now. Since I can only keep liquids in me, I've been drinking smoothies and shakes to help take the hunger away and have a bit of energy for my three LIVELY kids.

Corbin, Calvin, and Taylor are all flourishing and growing before me! I wish I could keep them this little forever. I can't believe Corbin is 10, Calvin is 5, and Taylor is 3! Where has the time gone?! I love each and every one of my babies, and in times where I'm feeling like this, they're such a breath of fresh air. I love Tyler's relationship with each of them; he treats them like they're his own flesh and blood. Corbin has even started calling him "Daddy" now. It took him longer to warm up to him than it did for

Calvin and Taylor. I feel bad that Tyler doesn't have any kids of his own, but I'm DONE having kids...three is enough for me! Tyler's playing with them outside, but we've got to get them to Mama's house because he's making me go to the doctor today. Aaron was supposed to get them to have them for the weekend, but once again, he fell through with his promise. I'm really starting to get sick of him! Let me pray:

> *God help me! Help me to forgive Aaron for all he's done and what he's doing to his children. Help his children to forgive him and not think differently or ill of him. No matter what he does, let me always uphold him and speak of him with respect to my children. Forgive him for he knows not what he's doing to them and their relationship. In Jesus' name, amen.*

We dropped them off at Mama's house, and they were all excited to be with her and their uncles. I dreaded going to the doctor because the last time I was in the doctor's office, I learned Daddy had passed and went to be with Jesus. Bittersweet, right?! But I needed to go to find out what was going on with me. Tyler grabbed my hand and held it as he drove us there.

"I know you don't want to go because of the memories it brings back, but you've got to so we can figure out what's wrong and how to help you get better."

"I know," I pouted.

"We've got three beautiful babies that need their mother...I need you. We love you and want what's best for you," he said as he kissed my hand.

"I know...I love you too, and I thank you for this; thanks for always pushing me."

"I'm always gonna be here for you."

We arrived at the doctor's office and waited in the waiting room for what seemed like forever. I know I probably over-exaggerate, and I don't know if you can tell, but I really don't like waiting. It's just one of those things I hate to do because it's hard to do. Maybe that's why God *ALWAYS* makes me wait because I don't like to, LOL. But He's constantly teaching me how to be patient.

They finally called my name, and Tyler and I walked back to the examination room.

"Dr. Riles will be with you in a moment," The nurse said.

Great, *more* waiting. After a while, Dr. Riles walked in.

"Hi, Tasha! It's been a while since we've seen each other. We're going to run some blood work on you to figure out what's wrong and get you fixed up, okay?"

"Okay!"

"Loss of appetite and weight loss. I'm thinking I know what it is, but we're going to do the bloodwork to check and be sure, okay?"

"Okay," I said as she proceeded to do the bloodwork. I wonder what she thinks is wrong because I haveth not a clue! Tyler held my hand during the entire process.

"Any questions?"

"Yes, Dr. Riles, what do you think could be wrong?" Tyler asked.

"Well, we're going to check her for Lupus."

"LUPUS?!" I said.

"I'm not saying you do or don't have it. That's why we're going to get you checked out, sweetheart. I'm going to go run the tests, and I'll be back shortly with the results, okay? You just hang tight."

Tyler began to pray.

Dear Lord, we thank You for this day. Thank You for life, health, and strength. God, I thank You for the family You have blessed me with Corbin, Calvin, Taylor, and Tasha. God, I thank You for Tasha's healing. I thank You in advance that the test for Lupus will come back NEGATIVE in Jesus' name. I thank You that ALL will be well with

Tasha, and she has no reason to fear because You're with her; You're with us EVERY step of the way. As we await to hear GOOD news, we ask for Your peace: the peace that surpasses ALL understanding. You promised to keep us in Your perfect peace as we keep our minds focused and stayed on You. We thank you now Lord, in Jesus' matchless name, we pray, amen.

"Amen," I said.

Tyler hugged me and continued to hold my hand. I know I don't have Lupus; there's no doubt in my mind about that. I'm not completely sure what's wrong, but I know it's not that! We waited in that room for two hours, and we were now both extremely hungry. Tyler went to the cafeteria and brought me back a sandwich and a smoothie. I could not eat the sandwich, but I do thank God I was able to drink the smoothie! Another hour passed, and then Dr. Riles finally walked back into the room.

"I'm sorry for you guys' long wait, but I have some very exciting news!"

"I don't have Lupus!" I said.

"Correct, you don't have Lupus!" Dr. Riles said.

"HALLELUJAH! PRAISE GOD!" Tyler exclaimed.

"YOU'RE PREGNANT!" Dr. Riles screamed excitedly.

"WHAT?!" I asked.

"What?! Really?! Wow! And Thank God!" Tyler said as he grabbed me to hug me.

How can this be possible? I said I was done having kids! Lord, three was more than enough for me...now four?! *God help me!*

"You're ten weeks to be exact!"

I was at a loss for words. Now didn't seem like the ideal time to be having another baby, but nonetheless, to God be the glory.

"That explains all of the nausea, grumpiness, and pain!" Tyler said.

Grump...well, I have been grumpy lately, LOL.

"I want to see you back for your twelve-week check-up, and then we can find out the gender, okay? Congratulations, you two!"

"Thank you so much, Dr. Riles!" Tyler said as we exited.

When we got outside to the parking lot Tyler picked me up and twirled me around. He was really excited as this would be his first biological child.

"I love you so much, baby," he said.

"I love you too!" I replied.

"Wow! I can't believe I'm having my first official child?!" he said. "I mean, Corbin, Calvin, and Taylor are mine, but..."

"I know what you mean; it is exciting," I said, trying to sound happy with and for him despite how I was feeling. I know this too shall pass, and as time progresses, I'll be more than excited to meet our baby boy or girl.

"I can't wait to tell everyone! Should we wait until after the first trimester?" Tyler asked.

"It just depends on *who* you want to tell," I said.

"TRUE! We can trust your mama and 'nem," he said.

We arrived at Mama's house, and Tyler was just bursting with joy and excitement! It was really cute and sweet to see.

"What did the doctor say?" Mama asked.

Tyler couldn't stop grinning.

"It's obviously good news since Tyler came in here grinnin' like a fool," Scott said.

"Well, what did she say?" Travis asked.

"We're pregnant!" we said at the same time.

"*Again?!*" Scott exclaimed.

Mama jumped up and hugged both of us. My brothers looked like they didn't know what to do. Tyler grabbed Corbin, Calvin, and Taylor so that we could explain to them what was going on. Their confused faces were hilarious!

"Mommy's having a baby, so that means, Corbin, you and Calvin are going to be big brothers again, and Taylor's going to be a big sister!" Tyler said.

I realized that Corbin was holding a phone to his ear. I wonder who he was talking to. I could hear, "WHAT?! Corbin let me speak to your mother!" as he handed me the phone.

"Hello?"

"Yeah, it's Aaron...You're pregnant?! Like you're really married to that man and having his child?! Two can play that game," he said as he hung up on me. I was frazzled.

"You okay, baby?" Tyler asked.

"That was Aaron, and he heard our announcement. I don't know why, but he's really upset."

I mouthed the word CRAZY to the adults in the room so I wouldn't speak ill of my kids' father in front of them.

"Yeah, well, I'm happy for y'all and all, but my initial reaction was 'again?!'" AJ said as he laughed.

CHAPTER SEVEN
Who Could It Be?

Things have gotten crazy since we told both of our families our good news. Tyler's family started reaching out and coming around more, especially his parents. They were especially excited as this would be their first official grandchild, which I thought was nice. But the weird thing is that Aaron won't stop calling and coming around now. He went from being on a hiatus to showing up at random times of the day and calling at random times of the night. To be honest, I liked it better when he didn't call at all! He's been spending more time with the kids, which is good, but he doesn't bring them back when he's supposed to. I'm not sure if I should allow myself to be happy about that or if I should let it bother me. Tyler and I have talked about it, and we've prayed about what we should do and how we should address Aaron, but we haven't gotten a revelation yet, so we'll wait on God.

I'm going to the doctor today for my twelve-week check-up, and we find out the baby's gender, which is super exciting! I'm feeling totally different about this pregnancy now than I did when I first found out. Tyler is hoping for a boy to name after himself, but I'm hoping for a girl to even things out. As I was thinking about this, Darrell called me.

"Hey bro, how are ya?" I asked.

"Hey, lil' sis! I'm good, how about you?"

"Good and excited! We find out the baby's gender today!"

"Yeah, that's what I was calling about...God gave me a revelation about your kids."

"What did He say?" I asked.

"Tasha, you're going to have a boy, and you're going to name him Trey after our brother. Don't worry, he's going to be *nothing* like our brother, in fact, he'll be the complete opposite. He's going to be very musically inclined, gifted, talented, and most important, anointed. A few years down the road, you'll have two more boys. One you will name after Tyler, and the other you will name Chandler. All your children are and will be anointed, and they'll go to higher heights, and deeper depths in God than any of us have. I see them forming a Christian band. Corbin is at the head of it, so maybe he'll start it, I'm not sure, but they will all lead worship together. Although they have different fathers, they're still going to be really close, and it's going to be as if they all come from the same man, but they actually do because they all came from God. You said you were done, BUT GOD ISN'T. Let Him do what He wants, and allow Him to accomplish what He wants, how He wants, through you and your family. You and Tyler are immeasurably blessed. God has great things in store for you both."

Wow! Two more kids after this one?! SIX kids total? Okay, God. Not my will, but Thine will be done!

"Lord, my! I'm honestly at a loss for words right now, Especially the SIX kids part!"

"It may seem like a lot, but God wouldn't give you more than you can handle, sis. Trust me. He's got a plan!"

"I would just like to say that I am super proud of how spiritually inclined and mature you are! I'm proud of how far you've come in the Lord. Darrell, like seriously, I see the shift, and He's about to lift you and take you even higher in Him!"

"I feel that and see it too, and to be honest, I'm *terrified*!"

"Darrell, this literally just came to me. The mantle has been passed from Daddy to you! You're the new pastor of Deliverance Church!"

I didn't hear anything for a while after I said that.

"Darrell?? You still there??" I asked.

"Yeah, I'm here…the crazy thing is…and I haven't told anyone so you're the *first* to hear it, okay?"

"Okay…what is it?"

"Daddy saw this coming. Before he got really sick, he took me aside and told me there was an anointing on my life. In fact, he said the same anointing that was on him was coming onto me. He told me I was going to take over Deliverance Church for him because he was no longer able."

I was in COMPLETE SHOCK! Why was this my first-time hearing this?!

"Tasha, I wrestled and wrestled with this thing. I begged God to choose someone else and take this cup from me. I saw how Daddy battled with all kinds of spirits and people. Shepherding and pastoring is no joke! It's heavy, it's deep, and I just wanna do right by God's sheep. But God told me to surrender, so I did…so now I'm just waiting on Him to reveal His decision to everyone else."

"Maybe God wants *you* to tell them?" I suggested.

"I don't know. I'll go back in prayer about it. But I do ask that you keep me lifted."

"For sure, got you covered!"

"Oh, and don't worry about Aaron. God hasn't told me what's going on with him yet, but He did say you'd find out, and He'd show you soon. I love you, sis. Take care."

"Love you too!"

Then we hung up.

WOW! Darrell is the new leader of Deliverance Church! I can't believe it! I'm so proud of him and what God is doing through him! I wonder what is going on with Aaron that's making him act so nutty, well nuttier than usual. I'll have to figure that out later because it's time for my doctor's appointment.

"Tasha, I'm heading to the car!" Tyler yelled from downstairs.

"Okay, bae. I'm coming!"

As I got into the car, I couldn't help but feel joy; like I was super cheerful!

"I'm happy to see you happy!" Tyler said. "A complete turnaround from when we first found out about the baby. Do you think it's a boy or a girl?"

"It's a boy. Darrell just called and said God told him it's a boy, and we're to name him Trey, but he'll be *nothing* like my brother Trey…and then we'll have two more boys. One will be named after you, and the other will be named Chandler. So, we'll have three kids with names that start with the letter C and three with names that start with the letter T."

"My God! SIX kids?!" Tyler asked.

"Six," I said.

"To God be the glory," he said.

And sure enough, we went to the doctor and found out what we already knew: we were having a boy. Amidst all the excitement, we received a very disturbing letter in the mail. It was a death threat on me and Tyler. There was no name listed and no return address. But whoever it is knows us and knows where we live. Why would someone want to harm us? Who would want to harm us? Who could it be?

CHAPTER EIGHT
Too Much

It's been about two months since we found out we were expecting a baby boy, which is exciting! But this has also been a stressful time because we literally have less than a month to make the announcement about who the new leader of Deliverance Church will be, and Tina and Rhonda have been the absolute worst! Darrell wasn't kidding when he said he wanted God to take this cup from him because he hasn't shared any of what he told me to anyone else. Could it be he's waiting on God, but God's waiting on him? I can tell he really doesn't want this, but I see so much greatness within. It's time for him to come out of hiding. Peoples' lives and freedom really do depend on it.

To top off all of the drama that's been happening at church, Tyler and I were still getting death threats, and Aaron has been acting more of a fool than usual! With the way he's been acting, it wouldn't surprise me if he was the one sending us the death threats. When he calls, all he talks about is the fact that he hates Tyler and says mean things about me being pregnant. The last couple of times he's come to see the kids, his mama was with him, driving for him, which is unusual because she hasn't driven him around since he was a kid. I can't think about all of this right now because we have a meeting with the leadership board in less than thirty minutes. I don't know what else to do but pray.

God, thank You for everything You have given me. I'm so undeserving but You see fit to keep on blessing me. God, I thank You for all my children, a healthy pregnancy, labor, delivery, and a healthy baby boy. Thank You for Tyler and all that he is and does for this family. Thank you for reconciling us with Tyler's family. God, I ask that You go before us and this meeting with the leadership board today. Allow everything to go well, relieve me of all stress, and calm my fears. Lord, allow Darrell to rise up, walk in the authority You have given him, and take his rightful place. You've anointed him for this, and You've equipped him for this. We curse anxiety and fear right now in the name of Jesus. For You have not given us the spirit of fear but of love, power, and a sound mind. You tell us that in 2 Timothy 1:7. Let Darrell walk in Your anointing and power and be the fearless leader You've destined him to be all along. In Jesus' mighty name, I pray, amen.

We arrived at the church for the meeting, and although they weren't invited, Tina and Rhonda arrived at the same time as us. They just have this wicked demeanor about themselves, and it's very creepy. Don't they get tired and exhausted from wreaking havoc, causing unnecessary drama, and irritating others all day? Like isn't that exhausting? Seems like it would be to me!

Pastor Dawson was waiting for us in the church's conference room.

"Hey family, how are we doing today?" Pastor Dawson asked.

"Hey Pastor D, no complaints here," Mama said.

"And congratulations to you two!" Pastor D said as he looked at me and Tyler.

"Thank you!" we both said at the same time.

"I know that God has finally revealed to me who our new shepherd should be, and I believe He's revealed it to all of you too," Pastor D said, nodding at Darrell.

Both Tina and Rhonda rolled their eyes. Darrell looked down at the ground. Despite Mama's urging for them to stay home, AJ, Scott, Travis, and Trey came too.

"He told y'all? Cause I don't know nothin'!" AJ said. Mama gave him a firm yet gentle shove.

"Let's start this meeting off the right way, though—in prayer," Pastor D said.

Dear Lord, we thank You for this day. Thank You for breathing Your breath of life through us and for giving us another chance to pray. Father, I thank You for revealing to us who our new shepherd should be. Thank You for emboldening him, raising him up, and allowing him to walk in Your power. You've given him love, power, and a sound mind, God. Let him not be afraid to step out and answer the call from you, Lord. Let him know that he is spiritually equipped. He's been anointed and built for such a time as this! His weapons are not carnal, but mighty through You, God, for the pulling down of strongholds. You tell us that in Your word in 2 Corinthians 10:4. Let him not be afraid but be bold and courageous. Let him steward and lead Your people well. In Jesus' mighty name, we pray, amen.

We all said, "Amen."

"We all know what we're here to discuss and Who we're doing it for. I think this will be a fairly short meeting," Pastor D said. "Darrell, it's time to rise up and take your place. The anointing that was on your father is now on you; the mantle has been passed down to you, son. God wouldn't assign you to do something that you couldn't do or handle," Pastor D said.

"You've been waiting on God, but all this time, God has been waiting on you, baby," Mama said.

"Well, what do you say?" Pastor D asked as we all looked at Darrell.

"Wait, Darrell, you's a preacha now??" Scott asked as mama shoved him.

"HUSH Scott; and AJ don't you even open your mouth. You look like you was 'bout to say somethin' stupid! Darrell, what do you say, son?" Mama asked.

"I...well...I say yes. I've known for quite some time because before Daddy passed, he actually said the same exact words to me that you just spoke, Pastor D. I've been wrestling with it and wrestling with it. I mean, I gave God *every* lame excuse I could think of, from not having a wife to be the first lady to never having preached a sermon a day in my life. But God has really been dealing with me and allowing me to walk in the prophetic. It's time I stop running from what He's called me to and start running to Him. My answer will be yes, Lord. Yes!" Darrell said.

"HALLELUJAH! GLORY BE TO GOD! Well, folks, I'll finish out this month, and then next month, our new fearless leader can take it from here! No doubt you're making God proud, and I know your daddy would be super proud of you too," Pastor D said as he hugged Darrell.

Tina and Rhonda went storming out of the church. I mean, they really thought they were finna be the leaders of Deliverance Church!

Maybe this means they'll leave for good now, and the church can finally be at peace. Pastor D and Darrell stayed at the church to talk further with Mama while the rest of us left. As soon as I got in the car, my phone began to ring. It was an unknown number, but I decided to answer it anyway.

"Hello?"

"Hey, Tasha, this is Mama Campbell. I know it's been a few years since we've talked. How are you?" she asked.

The flesh wanted me to hang up immediately after hearing who it was, I was speaking to. The Holy Spirit said, "Nah, listen to what she's got to say." It took every bit of Jesus in me to not hang straight up on her.

"Hello? Hello? Tasha?" Mama Campbell said.

"Hi, I'm well. How are you?" I asked, unbothered.

"Not so good. That ole boy of mine has turned into a complete fool!" she said.

Yeah, no kidding! She's just realizing this?! I listened further as she talked.

"I realized that he's been sending y'all death threats. All he's been talking about is how he hates you and Tyler being together while he's snortin' something up his nose, smoking, and drinking. The boy's got a real big problem! I also found out he's got two other sons by some woman named Alex. They're around the same age as Corbin and Calvin, so he been cheatin' all along...every time I look some strange girl callin' talkin' bout he needs to step up and take care of his responsibility. Who knows how many kids the boy got!" she said.

Wait, Aaron was the one sending us death threats?! I mean, I figured it was him, but I wanted to give him the benefit of the doubt! Two other kids? Now it makes sense that every time he gets them, there are always two little boys in the car with him. He and I are no longer together, and I've moved on, so I can't even be mad at that. But drugs? The fool is on drugs? That explains why he's acting nuttier than usual. God help him!

"Tasha, you there, honey?" Mama Campbell asked.

"I'm here...that was just a lot to take in," I said.

"I know it is, baby. I could hardly believe it myself. I'm sorry I neglected you and my grandbabies in y'alls time of need. I really am sorry about that! The boy told me all kinda crazy things about you; might've been brainwashed even! He's just not right. HE'S JUST NOT RIGHT! Can't even leave him in the house alone by himself, just crazy; nuts even!" she said.

Well, that explains why she's been coming around with him and driving for him. It's all starting to make sense now.

"I saw how you helped to save him from that ole wicked Felicia, and I know I can trust you with this information. I'm trying to get him in a rehab, but he grown, and I can't tell him nothin'. I know you's a praying woman, and you got yourself a praying man now. Please, please, please pray for my boy. Pray that God would truly save him, deliver him, and get him off them drugs! This is too much for me, Tasha, too much!" she said as she began to cry.

"You know what, Mama Campbell, let's pray right now," I said.

Tyler looked shocked to hear the name of who I was speaking to.

Dear Lord, we thank You for life, health, strength, and the activity of our limbs. Thank You, Lord, for giving Mama Campbell revelation, and for allowing her to see the error in her ways. Thank You for forgiving us all of our sins and reconciling us back together again. God, we come before You lifting Aaron up to You. Lord save him, really save him and get him off of this path of self-destruction. Deliver him from alcohol, drugs, sex, and cigarettes Father. Let him want to be better, not only for his children, but for himself as well. Let him be willing to go into rehab and get help, Father. SAVE him God, save him! HEAL him Father as You are Jehovah Rapha, the God that healeth thee. And strengthen Mama Campbell as she tries to help him along the way. SAVE her too and let her know that You DO hear her when she prays. We believe Your word and we ask that You honor this prayer. In Jesus' matchless and mighty name, we pray, amen.

"Thank ya, baby. I feel better already!" Mama Campbell said.

"Thank you for calling! Please keep me updated."

"Will do! Oh, he's coming into the room now, talk to you soon!" she said as we hung up.

Tyler looked shocked at what just took place.

"Bae, that explains a *whole* lot!" he said.

"I know! Just keep them lifted in prayer."

"Fa sho."

Wow, I can't believe all that I just heard! Lord, I know You hear me when I pray, so please be gracious and kind to answer my prayer. Lord, I can't deal! I can't, but *YOU* can! This is too much, God. Too much.

CHAPTER NINE
Stepping Up

It's been a couple of months since I've heard from Aaron and Mama Campbell. Maybe she was able to get him into a rehab facility? I'm not sure. But Darrell has been killin' it at the church! Every time he ministers, I'm like, "Is this my brother?" Especially this past Sunday. My God! The boy is anointed. As each day passes by, I get more and more excited to meet baby Trey. I can't tell who's more excited, my in-laws or Tyler. Mama Washington has been calling to check on us and coming by non-stop, which is so nice being that at one point in time, they (my in-laws) resented me, and Tyler and I's relationship. God has brought us all a mighty long way!

It's now time to pick the kids up from school, and since I promised to take them out for ice cream this afternoon, both Tyler and I went to go get them. We pulled up to the parent pick-up line, only to find that our kids weren't there.

"Why aren't they out here?!" I asked.

"Maybe one of our mamas thought it was their day to pick them up?" Tyler suggested.

We both dialed our parents to find out that neither of them picked up the kids. We then parked the car in the school's parking lot to go into the office and see what was going on.

"Good afternoon, Mrs. Clark. I hope your day was great. Calvin, Corbin, nor Taylor was in the parent pick-up line. Are they still in their classrooms?" I asked.

"No ma'am, their father, Mr. Campbell, signed them out early today. He said he already ran that by you all," Mrs. Clark said.

"He didn't run anything by us. We didn't know anything about this!" I said irritably.

"Ma'am, with all due respect, please make sure that you call either Tasha or me whenever something like this happens *before* you release them to anyone," Tyler interjected.

"I do apologize! His name was on the emergency list, so I honestly thought you all knew he was picking them up, and I thought everything was okay. My sincerest apologies! I do hope everything will be okay!" Mrs. Clark said.

"Thank you!" we both said as we hurried out of the door.

God, what is Aaron up to?! Why would he go MIA and then all of a sudden randomly get the kids without checking with me first? Lord, please keep my babies safe. I have no idea what state of mind he's in right now. Please keep my babies safe. Please, God, please keep my babies safe. In Jesus' name, amen.

"Everything's gonna be alright, baby. You try and get a hold of Mama Campbell, while I try to get a hold of Aaron," Tyler said.

I dialed Mama Campbell, and each time, the phone kept going straight to voicemail.

"Hi Mama Campbell, it's Tasha. PLEASE give me a call back at your earliest convenience! I'm concerned Aaron may have run off with the kids. Please call me back!"

I left message after message but received no callback. Is she okay? The last time I spoke with her, she said Aaron was acting all nutty. Could he have done something to her? Is she hurt? No matter how many times Tyler called Aaron, he wouldn't pick up the phone either.

"Aaron, this isn't funny. We just want to know you and the kids are okay and safe. Please give either me or Tasha a callback," Tyler pleaded.

In times like this, I wish I had given Corbin a cellphone after all, even though he's only ten. Then the idea struck me; maybe I should try calling Aaron since he's not answering Tyler. I dialed him twice, and it went straight to voicemail each time. I heard the Holy Spirit tell me to try dialing him again, so I did, and this time, he picked up!

"Yeah, Tasha, why you and yo ole thing keep callin' me?!" Aaron said, sounding agitated.

"We just wanted to make sure you and the kids are okay, is all," I said.

"ME?! Shoooot...y'all don't care nothin' bout me nor my feelings. You got Tyler and Tyler got you. Who I got? NOBODY! Don't nobody care 'bout me!" Aaron said.

He sounds very depressed! I felt the urge to rebuke the spirit of suicide, so I did.

"Aaron, what are you talking about? We do care about you...been praying for you too."

"Yeah, right. I bet!" Aaron said.

He sounded like he was either high or drunk, or maybe a combination of both.

"Where are you?" I asked.

"Where I always am...duh! Don't worry. Our little brats are okay too. They're in the front room watching cartoons. You ain't foolin' me, Tasha. I know you ain't concerned about me. You just wanted to make sure I ain't do nothing to them kids. Well, guess what?! They're MY kids too. I ain't gone hurt 'em. I ain't gone hurt 'em," he said.

"Is it okay if I come by?" I asked.

"Yeah, guhl. I guess. Just leave the wife stealer AT HOME!" he exclaimed.

"Aaron, Tyler is *my* husband. He's going to come with me. We *both* care about you and want to make sure you're okay, is all."

"Um-hum...yeah, whatever. I'll be here waiting, except if I'm not. Ha ha ha ha," he laughed creepily.

Tyler and I hurried over to Aaron's house. We broke several speed limits, but glory be to God, we did not get stopped or pulled over. But I couldn't help but wonder what Aaron could be up to and what his motives were.

"Bae, this don't make no sense. No sense at all," Tyler said.

"I know, baby. He just needs prayer. LOTS and LOTS of prayer," I said.

We arrived at Aaron's house to see he left the door unlocked for us. Corbin, Calvin, and Taylor were in the living room watching TV and playing just like he said they were. They were playing with four other kids. The two little boys I would always see in the car when Aaron came to get them, and another little boy and girl. Aaron came out of the back with a cigarette hanging out of his mouth. He looked tired and worn out, like he hadn't slept in days.

"See, I told you they were fine. What's the big deal anyway?! Can't I pick up my kids whenever I feel like it? Or was that a problem with *you*, wife stealer?" he said, directed at Tyler.

"We just wanted to make sure everyone was okay. No, it's not a problem with me if you want to see and spend time with your kids because they're *your* kids. BUT it IS a problem when you randomly sign them out of school without notifying one of us. We were concerned because we thought something might've happened," Tyler explained.

"Yeah, yeah. You sound just like my other baby mamas! All y'all care about is the kids. The kids this, the kids that. Aaron, where's my child support? Aaron, you didn't do this, you didn't do that. Aaron, you're a terrible father. Aaron, stop making promises you can't keep. Aaron, you're such a disappointment. That's ALL I hear! I failed my marriage, married a woman that tried to kill me, cheated, and got all these kids. Don't NOBODY care 'bout me. Don't nobody care 'bout me. Lost my acting career, can't be no playwright no more, don't nobody want me. Don't you see? I got feelings too, but don't nobody care!" Aaron said as he began to weep.

Tyler and I looked at each other, and it was clear neither of us knew what we needed to do. So, we prayed.

Father God, we come before You lifting Aaron up to You, God. Lord, please cleanse him, purge him of all sin and unrighteousness. You shut the mouth of the enemy. He is who You say he is. Father, we ask that You wrap your loving arms around him, give him the comfort he needs. Let him know that You love him with an everlasting, unconditional love. Pornography, alcohol, and sex, we curse EVERY form of perversion that has tried to enter him. Clean him up, Lord! Only You can do it! Save him and make him white as snow. Show him Your unconditional, never- ending, relentless, agape love. You left the ninety-nine just to get to him, the one. Father, have Your way, and do what only You can do. In Jesus' perfect and mighty name, we pray, amen.

After Tyler offered up that prayer, Aaron literally fell into Tyler's arms and wept. I made sure all of the kids were okay, and they were, thank God. They just expressed they were hungry because they didn't have lunch at school. I could hear Mama Campbell screaming from one of the back rooms.

"TYLER!? TASHA!? Is that you? AARON, LET ME OUT OF HERE!" she screamed.

"Mama Campbell? Where are you?" I asked.

I didn't hear anything after that.

"Aaron, where's your mom?" I asked.

Aaron held his head down and said, "She's in her room...in the closet."

"IN THE CLOSET?! WHY is she in the closet?" I asked as I went to go find her.

"I locked her in there 'cause she kept stressin' me out and tryna tell me what to do!" he answered.

I immediately found her and unlocked the closet door to release her.

"Thank God you're here! I told you that boy been crazy. I been locked in that closet for six hours!" she yelled. "He needs help!"

"Aaron, we've got to get you some help. This isn't the way at all. I know we prayed, and we believe the prayer, but faith without works is DEAD. We need to get you enrolled in rehab ASAP. You gotta get better for you and your kids. They deserve to have the best version of you, and you do too," I said.

"So, what do you say?" Tyler asked.

"Alright! I'll get some help," Aaron whimpered.

"PRAISE JESUS!" Mama Campbell said.

Tyler and I loaded Corbin, Calvin, and Taylor into our car while Mama Campbell took Aaron and the other kids in hers. We followed them to the White Water Springs Rehab facility, where Aaron willingly checked in to get help.

"I want this to be clear; I'm doing this to be a better man for my kids. I wanna be better so I can step up. I gotta step it up for them," he said.

CHAPTER TEN
Whew Chile

Whew, chile. That may have been one of the craziest things I've ever experienced, but I'm so glad Aaron is *finally* getting help. He's in rehab, and he's getting counseling as well. Shoot, I might even need counseling after all this, LOL, but no for real, God has brought me through so much; He's brought us through SO MUCH! Despite all the chaos around us, Tyler and I have been doing everything in our power to prepare for Baby Trey as he'll be here in less than four months. I'm experiencing a whirlwind of emotions right now; I mean, my hormones are all out of whack, and I can't stop crying. Baby Trey has been making me super emotional.

Church has been very peaceful for the most part. That group that Tina and Rhonda got riled up still been trippin' about Darrell becoming the senior pastor. I guess everything can't always be peaches and cream. But, from what I've seen and to my knowledge, it hasn't fazed him. He's been pushing through the opposition and doing what God has called him to do. If you didn't know and if you can't tell, I'm one proud sister! Tina hasn't come back to the church since she stormed out of the meeting a few months ago, but Rhonda has tried to slither her way back in, and it's been really weird. I don't know if it's just me, but it seems like she's been after Darrell.

Every time I look, it's like she's just about falling at his feet. Always needing this or that or requesting prayer for what seems like the silliest of things. Last Sunday, for example, she got a paper cut from her church program and went running up to him, demanding he laid hands on her so she could be healed. Ridiculous, right?! To me, she reeks of desperation. I'm wondering when exactly she started crushing on him because she's never paid him any attention before. Like, she wasn't thinking about him all along, so what's changed now? The only thing that's changed is his title. I'm wondering if he's noticed it, or if he's just being nice by not saying anything? Welp, here's my opportunity to ask him because he's calling me now.

"What's goin' on, Mr. Preacha Man?" I teased.

"Lil' sis! What up tho?! How ya been?" he asked.

"Great! Preparing for Baby Trey day by day. How about you?" I asked.

He hesitated.

"I'm... good."

"Um-hum. What is it?"

"You sound just like Mama!" he exclaimed. "But you know how I mentioned I'd been desiring female companionship?"

"Shut yo mouth and keep on talkin'! This is the *first* time I'm hearing about any of this!"

"Oh, right. I mentioned it to AJ and 'nem, which was a bad mistake. Horrible! I mean, that was the *worst* conversation of my life!"

"Now, you know better than to try to talk to them about that...but what's up?"

"True. I should've talked to Tyler about it or you first. But, yeah, so I've been battling with loneliness lately, and I've been praying hard to God about it. I mean, I thought He wanted me to be like my homies in the Bible and live the consecrated/sabbatical life. But He did tell me He'd show me my wife, when it was time, though."

"What you're feeling is normal, just stay focused, rooted, and grounded in Jesus. That's what's helped me when I felt that way before Tyler and I got together. And if God said He'd show you her when it's time, then what's the problem?"

"The problem is that Rhonda won't leave me alone!" he began.

Here we go, I thought.

"*Who* gave the woman my cellphone number?! I know I sure didn't! She calls me at the most *random* times about the *stupidest* things! Yesterday she called me because she couldn't find her car keys, right, and get this...she wanted *me* to come over to her house and pray with her that she'd find them. She literally wanted me to come over for that! Like is she okay? She's *always* all up under me, and at church, I know you see her; she's always at the altar for something. Don't get me wrong, I want people to be prayed for and get their deliverance, but you gotta be up at the altar *every* Wednesday night, Friday night, and Sunday morning? Come on now!"

I couldn't help but laugh because this was *hilarious* to me!

"You're laughing, but I'm at my wits end with this mess. At first, I thought maybe, just maybe, she could be her. But that lasted all of sixty seconds! If that's her way of trying to tell me she likes me, then my God. It was cute at first, but now it's just ridiculous! It seems like desperation to me. Did I mention it was ridiculous?!"

"Yes. Yes, you did," I said, still chuckling.

"I don't want to hurt her feelings, so what should I do? I feel like I need to handle this before I can begin to pursue..."

"You've just got to be honest and set boundaries. Be like, 'Listen, if you're going to call me, call me for emergencies only.' Let her know as her pastor, you are genuinely concerned about her well-being, but it's hard to believe her about anything when she's constantly crying wolf. Let her know you ain't gone be rippin' and runnin' over there for every little thing. She gotta put some respect on yo name! Put some prayer on it, ask for direction, and God will show you how to be firm yet gentle. Feel me?"

"I feel ya, and that's some sound advice, sis. Thank you!" he said with gratitude.

"Now, you mentioned pursuit...*who* is she?" I said curiously.

"Awe, here we go."

"No, seriously, I wanna know! Who's this mystery woman? Does she go to the church?"

"No, she does not go to the church. God made it clear the woman I'd marry wouldn't be a member of Deliverance Church. Her name's Carolyn. She's thirty, loves God, His people, and I think... she may be in love with me. Not sure if she is, she must be trying to see how things will go first. We've been seeing each other for about a month and a half now, but I didn't want to bring her around y'all until I knew for sure."

"Sounds like you *do* know for sure; you're just scared."

"You know me so well!"

"Does she know about the Rhonda issue?"

"Yeah, she was like, 'Look, that woman don't want no prayers, she wants you!' Yeah,

Carolyn's the one who made that clear for me, LOL," he chuckled.

"I like her already! And, *whenever* you're ready, I'd *love* to meet her."

"Thanks, sis! Thanks for being a listening ear and allowing me to vent. A lot of times, pastors are expected to be a listening ear, intercede for others, and shepherd them, and we're like, 'Well God, who's got us?' I know you got me, sis, and I love and appreciate you. My lady is calling, so I'll talk to you soon!"

"*Anytime*, bro. Anytime! I ride for you, homie. I always got your back. And by the way, I think it's smart to keep her away from AJ, Scott, Travis, and Trey. They'd run her off, LOL."

"No doubt about it!" he said as we hung up.

Wowzer! Darrell's got a lady friend! I'm so happy and excited for him, and I'll *finally* get a sister! I know Mama will be ecstatic, but AJ and 'nem. Whew chile, Darrell did the right thing by not bringing her around them.

CHAPTER ELEVEN
Babymoon

Remember when I mentioned Tyler and I didn't get to go on our honeymoon? Yeah, well, we decided to go on a babymoon instead! Since Baby Trey will be here in less than two months, instead of going to Hawaii, as we had planned, we decided to go to Santa Monica and spend a week there. It was really bittersweet because today, November 19th, would've been Daddy's seventy-sixth birthday. I miss him more and more as the days go by, but I know he's in a better place. Like, he's chillin' with Jesus, and knowing that he's in no more pain is all I could ever ask for. He's already up there with God, and I've got to get there. And there's no doubt I will because I am determined to hear God say, "Well done thy good and faithful servant, you've been faithful over a little, and I'll make you ruler over much, enter in the joy of the Lord" (Paraphrasing it).

It was hard to enjoy myself because I was thinking about Daddy, wondering how we'd be celebrating if he were still alive today. Don't get me wrong, Santa Monica is beautiful, and I'm glad to be sharing in this experience with Tyler, but part of me feels like I should be back in Palm Springs with Mama. This is her first time not being with Daddy on his birthday. This will be our first

Thanksgiving without him; first Christmas, first New Year, first everything without him, and I feel like I should be there for her. I know she has AJ, Scott, Darrell, Travis, and Trey (God help her with dealing with them), but I feel like I should be there too. She also has the kids there with her, and maybe they'll help keep her busy and take her mind off of things. I don't know; maybe I just need to focus on the good memories and times with Daddy and allow myself to have somewhat of a decent time while we're here.

We decided to go for a walk on the beach. The wind flowed through my hair, the sand squished between my toes as we walked, and I could smell the salty ocean water as the wind blew on my face. The sun was going down, and the view was absolutely breathtaking.

"It doesn't get any better than this," I said as I gazed into Tyler's eyes. He proceeded to kiss me. This is the most relaxed I have been in a while and probably the most relaxed I'll be, being that Baby Trey will be here soon. The thought of juggling and parenting four kids terrifies me! I barely feel afloat with three. But, to God be the glory for sending me a man who holds it down when I feel like I can't.

We finished our walk and decided to head back to our hotel to freshen up and get ready for bed. I noticed I had three missed calls from

Mama Campbell, but she didn't leave any voice messages. *The kids are staying with my mom, so I wonder what she wanted,* I thought before dialing her back. The phone rang for a while and went straight to voicemail. Although I was sleepy and tired, I decided to try dialing her again, and this time she picked up.

"Hey Tasha...I'm sorry I called you on your honeymoon...I mean baby moon...whatcha call it."

"That's okay...is everything okay? You sound a little unsettled."

"That's because I am unsettled! *Very* unsettled at that! Oh, Tasha, I don't know what to do! I just don't know what to do!" Mama Campbell exclaimed.

"Well, I'd love to help, but you gotta give me a little bit more information."

"It's that ole boy of mine. I don't know what's wrong with him! He's just a nut, an idiot even! He takes after his ole no-good father. I don't know what's wrong with him. I raised that boy all by myself with only God to help me, and then he turns around and acts just plain ole fool. A fool, I tell you, A FOOL!" she went on.

I could tell by the way she was talking things were about to head south, but I won't let it put a damper on my mood! I was a tad agitated because it seems like we get a breakthrough with Aaron, and then he slips back into his old ways, but I continued listening to what she had to say.

"I mean, I tell you I don't know what to do 'bout that boy! I dropped him on his head a few times when he was a youngin' but he ain't never been this fool!"

"Well, Mama Campbell, what happened this time?" I asked, trying to understand what she was talking about.

Tyler rolled his eyes and mouthed, "What now?" as I shrugged my shoulders and proceeded to place her on speakerphone so he could hear.

"See, that boy got me rantin' and ravin' like I'm a fool! But here's the thing, Tasha, that boy done checked himself outta rehab, and run off to only God knows where. He didn't even complete his program! I think he enjoys actin' like a dingbat, I really do!"

There was an awkward silence because I really didn't know what to say.

Lord, how long? How many times do we have to keep going back and forth with Aaron? One minute he wants to be better and do right, the next   minute he's like a barbarian or uncultured swine. Lord, PLEASE touch his   heart and completely renew his mind. Romans 12:2 says for us not to be conformed to this world, but to be TRANSFORMED by the RENEWING OF OUR MINDS. God, I thank You for Aaron's mind renewal, I thank You in advance in Jesus' name, Amen.

"I felt in my spirit you was prayin' for my boy just now...and I thank you."

"Not a problem, just being obedient to God."

"Ya know, we didn't have all these issues when you two were together...he seemed more levelheaded back then 'cept for when he cheated and all with that ole Felicia. I wonder if whatever she was using to dope him up to kill him has his brain cooked up like this?"

"Oh, now let's not dwell in the past. Things between Aaron and I are exactly how they should be. We co-parent, and that's that on that."

"Yeah, I know...I was only sayin' that because when he was with you, he had somebody that was good, a keeper, helpmate, and a really good friend. YOU'RE GOLD, Tasha, and I know your new man Tyler knows that."

Tyler nodded his head at that part and smiled uncontrollably, LOL.

"Thank you, Mam—" I started as she interrupted.

"You welcome, baby! Now, as for me, I guess I better go file a missin' persons report because that boy ain't been stabilized. He ain't in his right mind and honest to God, I don't know where he's at."

"Do what you feel. Tyler and I will try calling him too."

"Alright! Thank ya, baby, and do let me know if you're able to reach him. In the meantime, I'll file a missing person's report for this crazy man," she said before hanging up.

Tyler and I both looked at each other in disbelief that Aaron was acting crazy *yet* again.

"I love Mama Campbell and all, and I'm happy to help in any way I can, but when is she going to realize you and Aaron are NOT getting back together?" Tyler asked.

"I don't know. The woman can dream, I guess," I said as I shrugged my shoulders.

"I do agree whatever Felicia gave him, and that stuff he was on has got him cooked! He ain't never been like this. I wonder what his deal is?"

"I don't know, he did lose his career...maybe he's just handling things the wrong way? All we can do is keep him lifted and trust God to do the rest," Tyler suggested.

"I did tell Mama Campbell we would try calling him."

"Let's do it," Tyler said.

The phone rang and rang before eventually going to voicemail. We tried calling him two more times before leaving a message.

"Aaron, it's Tyler and Tasha...this isn't funny. Your mother is worried sick about you. We just wanna know you're okay. Call one of us back soon, please! We just wanna know you're okay."

Your mother is worried about you!" I said.

Doesn't he get tired of going back and forth to the same old way? I thought he meant it the *second* time when he said he wanted to be better? We're too old to be playin' games. He's got like, I don't know, five kids. Lord, if he doesn't want to be better for himself, help him to want to be better for his kids. We packed up and got some rest because we were heading home the next morning. I'm going to enjoy sweet and peaceful rest tonight and then deal with the foolishness tomorrow.

CHAPTER TWELVE
What Now?

We checked out of our hotel room, loaded up the car, and headed back to Palm Springs. Despite the weird phone call last night, this really was a peaceful and relaxing trip. It was also much needed! My phone started ringing; I looked down at it and saw that it was Aaron. I answered, but as soon as I did, he hung up. He did this a total of five times, FIVE times! I don't have time for childish games. The only reason I answered each time was to try and see where he was for Mama Campbell's sake. He kept calling, but I didn't answer because I wasn't up for the games.

"Aaron called, but every time I picked up, he would hang up. Now he's ringin' my phone off the hook," I told Tyler.

"Answer one last time to see what he says," Tyler said.

Alright, here goes. "Hello, Aaron."

"Hi...Tasha... I see you answered this time."

"What are you talking about? I answered the first five times you called, but every time I answered, I could hear you laugh and hang up."

"Oh! Dang it! I didn't know you heard me laughing. I was only trying to have some fun. Even thought about prank calling you."

"Aaron? What's with the foolishness? You're a grown man...it's time out for games like that."

"I only wanted to have some fun! You try being locked up in a rehab facility and not be able to have the things that you love!" he screamed.

"Aaron, why did you check yourself out of rehab?"

"I wanted to have a bit of fun...a getaway if you will...like you and Tyler."

Tyler and I glanced at each other. Neither one of us had spoken to him prior to our trip, so we weren't exactly sure how he knew about it.

"Yeah, you're probably wondering how I knew what y'all were doing...my mama told me. She got a big mouth, huh?"

"Aaron, you ought not talk that way or speak ill of your mother," Tyler said.

"Why not? She always bad mouthin' me! Always callin' me stupid, dumb, or crazy. So, I decided to show her crazy!"

"I sent her on a wild goose chase and had her thinkin' I checked out of rehab. I BEEN here! I ain't leave, just told her that! Ha ha and she believed me! I guess I had her in a panic so much so, she ain't think of checkin' with the facility. And Wife Stealer, don't you tell me how I should talk!"

"Aaron, this is really too much for me right now! Why would you do that to your mother? Why would you make her worry like that?"

"She ain't worried 'bout me! She ain't even call the facility to see if I'm here. That don't seem like 'worry' to me!"

"The woman filed a missing person report!" Tyler said.

"Well, WHO files a missing person report BEFORE checking with everyone they know to see if they've heard from the person? Just because I CHOSE not to answer her phone calls, she calls y'all and thinks I've gone missing? And she say I'm dumb? Come on now!"

"Stop disrespecting her and call her to let her know you're okay and you haven't checked out of the facility!" I exclaimed.

"Yeah, yeah, whatever...I'll call her... I guess."

"You only get ONE mama, Aaron. Cherish her and respect her...Don't treat her like this. Love on her while you can before it's too late," I said.

"See, this is why I don't like talkin' to you sometimes...you be gettin' all deep...especially since your pops," Aaron started.

"DON'T EVEN go there," Tyler said.

"Alright, alright. That was too far...my condolences, Tasha. I know this is a hard time for you being it would've been his birthday and all. Thanks for the sound advice. I'll call my mama even though she be naggin' me all the time. I should be grateful to have her though. Give the kids my love," he said as we hung up.

"You think he gone do right?" Tyler asked.

"Imma call his mama and let her know that he's alright," I said.

We waited for Mama Campbell to pick up the phone.

"Hey Tasha, sorry it took me a while to pick up. I was chewing that ole boy of mine out! Can you believe he played me like that?!" she exclaimed.

"I'm sorry he did that to you, Mama Campbell. Tyler and I got on him about that."

"I was gonna file a missing person's report! Thank God I listened to Him and didn't do it!"

"He's a trip, huh?" Tyler said.

"Oh, I'll take him on a trip, alright! You just wait 'til I get done with him! Matter of fact, let me go so I can tell him off some more!"

"Mama Campbell...here's just a word of advice. Try being more kind in your speech about him and towards him. He takes that kind of stuff to heart and then retaliates. Your words do have power, and believe it or not, although you may think your helping, your words are actually hurting him the more. Just be mindful and be careful what you speak. Talk faith; speak those things that are not as though they were. If you continue to speak positively about Aaron and speak life over him, you'll eventually see the fruit of your lips," Tyler suggested.

"Wow! I guess I never realized that! Thank you for opening my eyes to this. I'm gonna call him and apologize," she said before hanging up.

"Between the two of them, I have a headache," Tyler said.

I chuckled, and I guess I chuckled too hard because shortly after that, my water broke! Thank God we made it back to town, but I didn't even have my hospital bag with me. I thought about putting it in the car, but I forgot it. I guess I should've listened to the Holy Spirit urging me to bring it with me. We called our parents to let them know we were on the way to the hospital.

After ten hours of being in labor, on November 23, 2002, Trey Maurice Washington was born! He weighed eight pounds and ten ounces. He was an absolute dream! Looking into his eyes easily made me forget the foolery that had taken place hours earlier. I truly am grateful to God for entrusting me and Tyler to care for our children, our blessings. I'm even grateful for Aaron, for although he's wild, he had a part in this too. I'm glad he and his mom were able to actually communicate their feelings to one another and not just talk at each other. As the times, seasons, and as the year comes to a close, I can't help but be thankful for it all. Everything I went through, I *had* to go through to get to where I'm at right now. I wouldn't trade any of it, even the hurt and the pain, because it was necessary. It was necessary for my growth; it was necessary for my journey, and I truly am grateful. I'm looking forward to this new adventure of being the Washington's party of six. And I can't wait to see all that God has in store. Cheers to love, memories, *new* opportunities, AND NEW BEGINNINGS!

Fast Forward to Present Day

Quite some time has passed since we last shared part of our lives with you. The last thing you've heard about us was Aaron being extra (per usual) and Trey being born. But a lot has happened and changed since then, so let's get you all caught up. We've since had two more sons: Tyler Jr. (16) and Chandler (13). Corbin is now 28 and is married to the beautiful Lauren Campbell, and they're getting ready to welcome their first child! I can't believe I'm about to be a grandma! More like a glam-ma, because your girl is too young for this, LOL. He has a record company in which he produces house named artists, and Calvin (23) and Taylor (19) are getting ready to release their first album together! Proud is an understatement! Oh, and Darrell, I can't forget to tell you about Darrell! He and Carolyn married, and they now have four kids of their own. Ain't God good y'all? Mama is doing fine, and so are AJ, Scott, Travis, and Trey.

We're very happy now, but things have been very rocky for us. I know, I know…we go from happy to sad and then back to happy…and we do that a lot. But that's a part of life, right? I mean, life is full of ups and downs. We have our high highs and then our low lows. And sometimes, the low points in life can really take a toll. But I serve a God who is more than able, and He comes through for me and my family *every single time*! We're better than we've ever been, and for that, I'm grateful! I think you guys have heard enough about me; now it's time for you to meet my niece, Kamryn.

MISUNDERSTOOD
A Sneak Peek

I don't fit in anywhere, not even with my family. I'm the youngest of four, and being that my dad's a preacher, everyone thinks we're just this cookie-cutter family. I'm tired of trying to fit other peoples' expectations of what a preacher's daughter should be and what she should look like, especially my mom's. She's always comparing me to my older sister Kayla. "Kayla does this, Kayla does that. Why can't you be like her?" she always says. That's the thing, though; I *don't* want to be like her. I just want to be me and be me unapologetically. So, what if I'm "hood" or tomboyish; that's my style, that's me. So, what if I only have mostly guys as friends, except for Keely, she's my absolute best friend, and sometimes, besides God, I feel like she's the only one that truly gets and understands me. My dad tries, but he's always busy with church, praying for people, or visiting the sick or people in need. Don't get me wrong, I think my dad is amazing, and what he's doing for God is amazing, but sometimes, he gets so consumed with the church, my mom, and my other siblings that it feels like he forgets about me. I'm always being overlooked, no matter how hard I try to please people. I guess I said all this to say, "Hi. My name is Kamryn, I'm sixteen years old, and I'm very MISUNDERSTOOD."

Read about Kamryn in "Misunderstood," which will be AVAILABLE SOON!

www.ingramcontent.com/pod-product-compliance
Lightning Source LLC
Chambersburg PA
CBHW030134260626
47156CB00008B/2944